Jeremy Strong

My Brother's Famous Bottom Goes Camping

Illustrated by Rowan Clifford

PUFFIN

This is for Dan, Jo, Sam and Ben,

and for campers and yurters everywhere

PUFFIN BOOKS

Published by the Penguin Group
Penguin Books Ltd, 80 Strand, London WC2R 0RL, England
Penguin Group (USA) Inc., 375 Hudson Street, New York, New York 10014, USA
Penguin Group (Canada), 90 Eglinton Avenue East, Suite 700, Toronto, Ontario, Canada M4P 2Y3
(a division of Pearson Penguin Canada Inc.)
Penguin Ireland, 25 St Stephen's Green, Dublin 2, Ireland (a division of Penguin Books Ltd)
Penguin Group (Australia), 250 Camberwell Road, Camberwell, Victoria 3124, Australia
(a division of Pearson Australia Group Pty Ltd)
Penguin Books India Pvt Ltd, 11 Community Centre, Panchsheel Park, New Delhi – 110 017, India
Penguin Group (NZ), 67 Apollo Drive, Rosedale, North Shore 0632, New Zealand
(a division of Pearson New Zealand Ltd)
Penguin Books (South Africa) (Pty) Ltd, 24 Sturdee Avenue, Rosebank, Johannesburg 2196, South Africa

Penguin Books Ltd, Registered Offices: 80 Strand, London WC2R 0RL, England

puffinbooks.com

First published 2008
014

Text copyright © Jeremy Strong, 2008
Illustrations copyright © Rowan Clifford, 2008
All rights reserved

The moral right of the author and illustrator has been asserted

Set in Baskerville MT
Made and printed in England by Clays Ltd, St Ives plc

British Library Cataloguing in Publication Data
A CIP catalogue record for this book is available from the British Library

ISBN: 978-0-141-32357-2

www.greenpenguin.co.uk

MIX
Paper from
responsible sources
FSC™ C018179

Penguin Books is committed to a sustainable
future for our business, our readers and our planet.
This book is made from Forest Stewardship
Council™ certified paper.

Contents

1. Captain Birdseye and Cecily Sprout!   1

2. The Two-legged Tent   10

3. Look Who's Come for Breakfast   22

4. What a Shower!   31

5. Who's Taking What?   43

6. Bitten by a Duck   53

7. Ice Screams   62

8. A Volcanic Eruption   72

9. And Here's Henry . . .   85

10. A Small Victory   96

11. Startling Events   106

1 Captain Birdseye and Cecily Sprout!

My sister's got a pet carrot. She has, really – a proper carroty carrot. It has green hair and she dresses it in Barbie doll clothes. My sister calls it Cecily Sprout.

'Because my friend at nursery is called Cecily,' she told Mum and me.

'Yeah, but Cecily's not a sprout,' I laughed.

'I think you mean Cecily Carrot,' suggested Mum, but Tomato shook her head firmly.

'No, I don't. I mean Sprout.' She clasped the vegetable doll close to her chest and whispered in the carrot's ear. 'You're a sprout, aren't you? Yes, you are.'

'Has your friend at nursery got green hair?' I asked.

'Stop teasing her!' Mum murmured with half a smile. 'Tomato's only three.'

Of course, you've guessed that the green hair is really leaves growing out of the carrot top, and you may be thinking my family must be vegetable mad. Why is my sister called Tomato, and why does she have a carrot-doll?

Well, first of all I have a twin brother and sister. My sister's called Tomato and my brother's name is Cheese. They do have proper names – James and Rebecca – but they were born in the back of a pizza delivery van and my dad called them

Cheese and Tomato. It was just a joke, but it kind of stuck and now everyone calls them that, even Granny and her husband, Lancelot.

As for the pet carrot, that was sort of my fault. We grow vegetables in the back garden and the other day I dug up this weird carrot. The top half was normal but the bottom half had split into what looked like two long, pointy legs. I showed it to Tomato and told her it was a dancing carrot-woman. And now she won't be parted from it. She got me to draw a little smiley face on paper. Then we cut it out and stuck it on the carrot.

We grow loads of stuff. It's like a mini-farm out the back, with a goat and chickens and a tortoise. I know you don't usually find tortoises on farms but my dad got him. Yes – that's the same dad who named the twins after his favourite pizza. My dad's daft. (And great fun!) Dad says that Schumacher (that's the tortoise) is the garden's security guard.

'We haven't had a single cabbage stolen since

we got him,' declared Dad.

'We never had cabbages stolen *before* we got him,' Mum pointed out.

My dad's good at thinking up names. He used to have a pet alligator called Crunchbag – don't ask! – and our pet goat is called Rubbish. (Guess what she eats!) He's named the chickens too. We only got them a few days ago – four hens and a cockerel. The hens are supposed to lay eggs, but they haven't produced a single one yet. I'm not sure what the cockerel is supposed to do. At the

moment all he does is wake up the whole street in the morning before it's even got light. Our neighbour Mr Tugg isn't too happy about that and keeps coming round to our house to show off his impressions of an exploding volcano. (In other words he gets very, VERY angry!)

Dad has named the cockerel Captain Birdseye, and he calls *all* the hens Chicken Nugget. He thinks that's very funny. Mum says it's cruel. Dad told her she was being silly because hens don't understand English. Mum said that was

just as well, because if hens *could* speak they'd tell Dad that he was a nasty, horrible man who ate chickens. Dad replied that she ate chickens too. Mum said yes, but she wasn't the one calling them Chicken Nugget. Then they started laughing. My mum and dad are always having daft arguments.

'Anyway,' Mum went on, 'you can't call *all* the hens Chicken Nugget. Maybe the twins can think of some names. Come to think of it, where have they got to? I thought they came outside with us.'

'They did,' I agreed. 'They went to look at the chickens.'

There was a startled squawk from the hen house and a hen came zooming out, half running, half flying and three-quarters falling over itself. There were several more protests from deep inside the coop and two more hens burst out into the pen. They looked upset and rather ruffled. Mum folded her arms.

'I think I know where the twins are,' she

muttered. 'Nicholas, you're just about small enough to get inside. Would you mind rescuing the hens from the clutches of the evil pizza twins?'

Honestly, I'm always having to rescue something in our house. If it's not the twins, it's the hens, and if it's not the hens it's my dad! I folded myself up as small as I could and squeezed into the hen house.

It was pretty gloomy inside but I soon spotted Cheese and Tomato. They were sitting on the birds' perch. Cheese had his arms firmly wrapped round the last hen and appeared to be introducing the poor creature to his sister's pet carrot.

'This is Cecily Sprout.' Cheese looked up and beamed at me. 'This is my hen, and she says Cecily Sprout can ride on her back.' Tomato tried to stick the carrot on the hen's back, but without success – surprise, surprise.

I groaned. Sometimes I think madness must run in my family. We all get it from Dad, probably. Not only is my whole family crazy, but I hardly dare mention Cheese's famous bottom. Did you know about that? Cheese has probably got the most famous bottom in the country. When he was one he used to make TV adverts for a nappy company.

His bottom has been seen by millions! (But that's another story!)

'Has your hen got a name?' I asked him.

'Poop,' grinned Cheese, pointing at Tomato's jeans. There was a dirty white-brown smear on one leg. It could only be – you know!

'Poop did that,' Cheese smiled. 'She's a super-dooper-pooper!' The twins burst into giggles.

So there we are. Cecily Sprout, the Barbie-carrot, has a new friend – a hen called Poop. As for the other hens, they're called Mavis Moppet, Beaky and Leaky. So now you've met everyone!

2 The Two-legged Tent

Boy, oh boy! What a rumpus – big time! We've had a fox in the garden. It was after the chickens, of course, in the middle of the night. Dad said he reckoned the fox fancied a five-course meal.

'It would have Captain Birdseye for starters, then Chicken Nugget One, then Chicken Nugget Two, then Chick–'

'Yes, Ron,' Mum cut in. 'We get the picture. There's no need to go through the whole menu.'

'Want a chicken nugget!' demanded Cheese.

'See what you've started?' Mum complained. 'I knew those hens would be trouble. It's all your fault.'

Dad's eyes boggled. 'My fault? How come?'

'You got the hens.'

'Yes, because you said you wanted some eggs,' Dad protested.

'Exactly. I wanted eggs, Ron. I sent you out to get some eggs and you came back with five chickens.'

'So? I got you eggs on a time delay. They'll be fresher that way – new-laid,' smiled Dad.

'And how many eggs have they laid so far? None. And now we have a fox. It may not have got any of the hens this time but it will be back. You can be sure of that, and then you can say goodbye to your hens, not to mention all the eggs they haven't even laid yet.'

Dad went stomping off wearing a dark frown on his face. It's best not to talk to him when he gets like that. I knew that frowny face. It didn't mean he was cross. He was thinking, and he was bound to come up with a plan sooner or later. He always does. My dad's clever like that.

Sure enough, he came stomping back an hour later and announced his brilliant plan. He was planning to keep guard over the hens all night.

'You can't stand out there right through the night,' Mum told him.

'I'll lie down,' said Dad.

'You can't lie down either, Mr Dopey-drawers. Suppose it rains?'

'I shall be safe and snug in my tent,' Dad said.

'What tent? You haven't got a tent.'

'Yes, I have. I shall use the twins' play-tent.'

Mum burst out laughing. 'It's for babies!' she giggled. 'It's too small for you, you . . . elephant!'

'Isn't!' scowled Dad.

Mum had to go off to another room, but we could still hear her laughing. Dad looked across at me.

'Don't pay any attention to your mother, Nicholas,' he said. 'She doesn't know what she's talking about. I'll show her. You wait and see. You'll be very impressed.' Dad nodded a lot, as if he was trying to convince himself that his plan would work. 'Oh, by the way,' he added suddenly, 'can I borrow your old water-gun? Foxes can't stand getting wet. They're like dogs, you know – they hate water.'

'Er, Dad? It's cats that aren't supposed to like water.'

'Really? Oh well, they're much like cats, foxes are. They both have long tails. If I had a long tail I wouldn't like to get it wet. Would you, Nick?'

'I might if I was a crocodile,' I pointed out, and Dad gave me a sharp look.

'The trouble with you, Nick,' he said, wagging

a finger at me, 'is that you go to school and you learn things and then you come home and upset me with what you know.'

I grinned back at him. 'You don't like me being right,' I said.

'Exactly,' Dad agreed. 'Now, can I borrow your water-splurter, or not?'

'Of course you can.'

So last night Dad set up the twins' little play-tent right beside the hen run. Then we all watched while he tried to squeeze inside.

'Daddy's too big,' said Tomato.

'Fat Daddy,' said Cheese.

'I am not fat!' shouted Dad. 'This tent is stupid. I've never seen such a small tent. A mouse couldn't go camping in this.'

Dad finally managed to make himself reasonably comfortable, even though his feet were sticking out of one end of the tent and his head and shoulders were sticking out at the other. The tent only covered a little bit in the middle.

'There,' said Dad. 'That's fine.'

The rest of us couldn't speak for laughing. You've never seen anything like it!

'All right, laugh if you must,' snapped Dad. 'I'll show you. When that fox comes he's going to get the biggest surprise of his life.'

'He certainly will when he sees you wearing a tent like a miniskirt!' shrieked Mum.

We left Dad to it. I went up to bed and fell asleep. And then, shortly after midnight, I was woken by the most dreadful noises and a bright light streaming through my curtains. I thought the Martians had invaded.

I whisked back the curtains and peered outside. A giant beam of light had flooded our garden. It came from next door. Mr Tugg is not only the world's angriest man, he also runs the local Neighbourhood Watch. He's always trying to get people arrested. I dropped a crisp on the pavement near his house last week and he tried to get me arrested for dropping litter. Then a pigeon waddled up and ate it. Mr Tugg was furious! He accused the pigeon of eating the evidence! I think he wanted to arrest the pigeon too.

Anyhow, Mr Tugg is very hot on security and he's got searchlights mounted at the front and back of his house. He switches them on if he thinks there are burglars around, and it looked like he'd spotted one in our garden.

Mr Tugg was chasing a tent on legs round and round the hen run, while the tent on legs kept spraying Mr Tugg with high-powered jets of water from my water-gun. Then Dad tried to

escape by dashing into the run and hiding behind the hen coop. Mr Tugg came roaring after him, slid on all the wet mud and went crashing into the hen house.

Hens came hurtling out, flapping and clucking as if the sky had fallen in on them. Mr Tugg threw himself on top of Dad, blew his whistle and tried to arrest him, while Dad made several useless attempts to get back on his feet.

After that the whole thing turned into the weirdest pyjama-party you can imagine. Mum rushed out of our house in her pyjamas, closely followed from next door by Mrs Tugg in her nightie. They dashed over and tried to separate the two mud-wrestlers. It wasn't long before they ended up in the mud too and that was when Mum finally snapped.

'STOPPPPP!!!' she bellowed.

The fighting ceased at once. At last Dad and Mr Tugg looked at each other properly for the first time.

'You idiot!' hissed Mr Tugg. 'I thought you were a burglar!'

'And I thought you were a fox,' Dad growled.

'Do I look like a fox?' cried Mr Tugg.

'No! You look like a hard-boiled egg with a moustache!'

'You're crazy!' roared Mr Tugg, trying to brush great wodges of mud off his clothes and only smearing it even further. 'I always knew you were off your head.'

And so it went on. It took Mum and Mrs Tugg ten minutes to get them calmed down. Eventually Mr Tugg was dragged back to his own house and my mum persuaded Dad he should come back into our house for the rest of the night.

After that everything was peaceful, at least until morning. Breakfast was a very quiet affair. Mum would hardly speak to Dad, she was still so

cross with him. Dad pretended he hadn't done
anything wrong.

'And besides,' he pointed out, 'the fox didn't
come back, did it? I told you I'd protect the hens,
and I did.'

Mum took a deep breath. 'I don't suppose
those hens will ever lay eggs now. First they
almost get eaten by a fox and then they have to
put up with you and Mr Tugg playing at cops
and robbers.'

Dad opened his mouth to protest but one look
at Mum's face told him he'd do a lot better to
keep quiet, so he did. However, I was wondering
what he would do next.

3 Look Who's Come for Breakfast

Dad's not very pleased with Mr Tugg.

'He's an interfering old moan-bag,' Dad complained as we put away the breakfast things. 'If he wanted to play at being a policeman why didn't he join the police force?'

'Perhaps he prefers a quiet life,' suggested Mum. 'He runs the local Neighbourhood Watch to help everyone protect their property.'

Dad snorted. 'No – he runs Neighbourhood Watch because he likes blowing whistles, waving torches and setting traps for burglars. I bet he was a boy scout when he was a kid and had so many badges he had to have a special jumper with extra sleeves to make room for them. Mr Goody-Goody, that's who he is. And why are you laughing at me?'

'I'm laughing at the idea of a jumper with extra sleeves.'

'Well, don't. It's cruel to laugh at a man when he's in pain. Have you seen the bruise I've got on my shin from when Mr Tugg pushed me into the hen house?'

'You said you slipped on the mud,' Mum reminded him.

'I slipped because I was pushed.' Dad rolled up a trouser leg to show off his bruise. 'Look at that. It's the size of a melon.'

Mum bent down to get a better look. 'Hmmm, more grape-sized, if you ask me,' she muttered, winking at me. 'I'm not surprised Mr Tugg wanted to arrest you, creeping about with a tent wrapped round your middle.'

'I thought I heard the fox and I got up to look but I couldn't get out of the tent fast enough so I had to stand there with it on. You can hardly blame me. The tent was too small.'

'Oh! It was the tent's fault?'

'Exactly,' Dad nodded, and then he brightened up. 'But it did give me a good idea.'

Mum's eyes narrowed. 'Oh dear. Now I'm really panicking,' she said. 'Your ideas are always off the planet.'

Dad smiled. 'That's because I'm a free-thinker. It's important to try and think differently. Anyhow, what I thought was why –' Dad broke off suddenly and frowned at something on the table. 'Am I right in thinking that there's a carrot sitting up at the table wearing dolls' clothes?'

'Yes,' said Mum.

'But it's a carrot,' Dad repeated.

'Yes. Her name is Cecily Sprout,' Mum told him.

'But it's a carrot,' Dad repeated.

'Yes. It's Tomato's latest doll.'

'But it's a carrot,' said Dad again.

'Yes, Ron, we all know it's a carrot. But for Tomato it is actually her favourite doll. Think of it as a free-thinking carrot – a carrot that has gone beyond the boundary of just being an

ordinary carrot, a carrot that has become almost a person. Tomato was giving her breakfast before you came down.'

Dad's eyes almost fell out of his face. 'She was giving a carrot breakfast? The whole family's bonkers. I think I'm the only sensible person here.'

Mum burst out laughing. 'That really takes the biscuit. Now, are you going to tell us your good idea or not?'

But we still didn't hear what it was because Tomato appeared in the kitchen pushing her toy wheelbarrow. 'Giving Cecily a ride,' she said, lifting the carrot-doll from the table and sitting her up in the wheelbarrow. 'We're going to the shops to get some lunch for Cecily.'

'I thought she'd only just had breakfast,' Dad muttered darkly.

'What does Cecily Sprout eat?' I asked, just out of curiosity.

'Fish and chips and chocolate scream,' Tomato

declared. She always says 'scream' instead of 'ice cream'. My sister began to wheel the carrot outside. She turned at the door and looked back at Dad.

'You brokened our tent,' she said accusingly. 'Bad Daddy.'

'Sorry,' muttered Dad. 'And you say "broke", not "brokened".'

'Yes, and you brokened a lettuce.'

'*Broke*,' repeated Dad. 'It got squashed a bit, that's all.'

'Yes, and you put mud on your clothes.'

'All right, I know,' growled Dad, looking more and more like the world's worst criminal.

'Yes, and Cheese says he can touch the moon from the top of the hen house.'

'Is that so?' Dad shook his head in disbelief. 'Hang on, what do you mean, from the top of the hen house? Cheese isn't on top of the hen house, is he?'

Tomato peered out through the open door and nodded solemnly. 'Yes, and he's standing up too. No, he isn't, he's just slidded off.'

There was a loud yelp from outside, a moment of silence and then an even louder wail went up. We all rushed to the rescue. Cheese was more surprised and cross than hurt, but Mum calmed him down with a biscuit.

'Who didn't shut the gate properly?' demanded Mum, looking accusingly at Dad.

Dad's face puckered. 'I want a biscuit too,' he moaned, trying to change the subject. 'Look at my bruise. Boo hoo. Want a biscuit.'

'Big baby,' laughed Tomato.

'Yes,' agreed Mum. 'Your dad is the biggest baby of all. And what we still don't know is what Big Baby's Big Idea is. Come on, we're bursting to hear what it is, aren't we, Nicholas?'

'Bursting,' I grinned, wondering what crazy scheme Dad had in mind now.

'Well, I think we all need a holiday.'

'Great!' I yelled.

'Heavens above, you've actually come up with a good idea for once,' Mum chuckled.

'I know. And I think we should all go camping,'
Dad went on.

Mum's smile vanished. 'You don't want us to
wear little tents like you did, do you?'

'No! I am thinking of proper camping, with
proper camping equipment. What do you
reckon?' Dad beamed at us.

'OK,' nodded Mum.

'It'll be brilliant!' I said.

4 What a Shower!

You should see what my dad's brought home!
You'll never guess, so I'll give you some clues.
It's blue and yellow and the roof goes up and
down. You can sleep inside it. You can even go to
the loo inside it. And it's not a tent, it's a tent on
wheels! Yep – it's a camper van!

'It's got four beds,' Dad boasted.

'There are five of us,' I said.

'Cheese and Tomato can share,' Dad explained, and he lifted the twins up into one of the beds. 'They'll be like sardines in a tin.'

'You mean a cheese and tomato sandwich, Dad,' I grinned.

Mum raised one eyebrow. 'You two are like peas in a pod,' she said. 'It's very worrying. I'm already living with a crazy loon and now my oldest child is getting just like him. Oh dear.'

Dad gave Mum a hug. 'You love it really,' he suggested.

'Geroff, you big lump,' she giggled. 'What's this cupboard for?' She pointed to a double-door wardrobe and opened it up. Magic! It wasn't a wardrobe at all – it was a proper cooker unit with a stove, an oven and grill and everything.

'Oh my!' said Mum, impressed. 'That *is* clever.'

'There's a fridge,' I added. 'And look here, a toilet.'

Mum gazed into the tiniest little room. 'Oh, dinky!'

'You can take a shower in there,' Dad said.

'You are ridiculous, Ron,' laughed Mum. 'There's no room for a shower. What am I supposed to do – stand upside down in the toilet bowl and flush it?'

Dad rolled his eyes. 'Now who's being ridiculous? You sit *on* the toilet. See that shower head above you? The water goes everywhere but eventually it drains away through the plughole down there.'

Mum wasn't convinced. 'Suppose I put the shower on by mistake, when what I really want to do is flush the loo?'

'Suppose we give you a brain transplant?' suggested Dad. 'Honestly, how can you muddle up the shower with the toilet flush?'

'I suppose I am being a bit fussy,' agreed Mum. She glanced round the inside of the van again and a smile crept on to her face. I knew she was impressed. This was the best thing that Dad had ever done. We went back indoors and talked over holiday plans for ages.

'Going camping!' shouted Cheese, while Tomato went racing round the room making big jumps and getting wilder and wilder until Mum caught her up in her arms and swept her off her feet.

'Camping!' she yelled, waving her carrot in Mum's face. 'Cecily Sprout says she likes camping.' Tomato squinted up at Mum. 'What is camping?' she asked.

'You'll soon see,' laughed Mum. 'It's going to be fun, and Cecily can come with us.'

'Yes,' nodded Dad. 'Good idea, because if we run out of food we can always –'

'NO, RON!' shouted Mum. 'That is not funny. Not when you're only three.'

'I'm not three,' protested Dad.

'You know exactly what I mean. Anyhow, sometimes I think you're more like a three-year-old than the twins.'

'Thanks a lot,' muttered Dad.

'And Poop can come too,' Cheese announced, with a bright smile, but Mum shook her head.

'No, I'm afraid not, darling. We can't take Poop as well.'

Cheese's face began to crumple. 'Poop come too. It's not fair. You said Tomato can take Cecily.'

'Yes, I know I said that, but Cecily Sprout is a carrot and it's all right to take carrots camping, but you can't take hens camping.'

Dad looked at Mum with astonishment. 'Excuse me? *It's all right to take carrots camping?*' he echoed. 'Are you mad?'

Tomato joined forces with her brother and waved Cecily at Mum. 'Poop is Cecily's friend and they'll both be sad. Look, Cecily Sprout is crying.' She began to make whimpering noises on behalf of the carrot.

'I'm sorry, we can't take a hen camping,' repeated Mum.

'Why not?' Tomato sniffed.

'Because they don't make tents for hens,' snapped Dad.

'Poop can sleep in my bed,' my brother said.

'All the hens have to stay here,' insisted Mum.

Tomato put the carrot to her ear. 'What's that? Sssh, Cecily is telling

36

me something. Cecily Sprout says you and Daddy are horrible and all the hens should go camping and people should make tents for them.'

Dad's eyebrows were climbing up his head.

'I can't believe I'm being told off by a carrot. I think I'll go and do something sensible in the garden.'

I followed him out. I wanted to know what we were going to do with our goat, Rubbish. She needs milking every day and I'm the one who does that.

'Granny and Lancelot can look after her,' said Dad. 'They've done it before.'

'What about the hens?' I added.

'I'll get your mother to talk to Mrs Tugg about that. She's a reasonable woman – unlike Grumblebum, her husband. The hens don't need much attention, and she likes them, apart from Captain Birdseye, but that's only because he crows in the morning and wakes her up.'

I rang Granny to tell her our news and she was so excited to hear about the camper van that she said she and Lancelot would come round straight away. Sure enough, a few minutes later we heard the familiar roar of their motorbike as they came up the road.

Lancelot pulled off his helmet and whipped the shades from his eyes. 'Wow!' he breathed. 'That is some motor!'

'It's got a shower,' Mum said proudly. 'But you have to stand in the toilet to use it.'

Granny looked confused. 'Why do you boil sand for the shower?'

'I beg your pardon?' asked Dad.

'You said you get sand and boil it,' Granny repeated.

I laughed. I knew what had happened. Granny is a bit deaf at times and she mistakes words. 'Gran! Gran! Mum said you STAND in the TOILET to use the shower.'

But Granny was still confused. 'She may very well have said that, Nicholas, but it still doesn't make sense. Why do you stand in the toilet if you want a shower? If I want a shower at home I stand in the shower, not in the toilet. I think that's rather horrible. I wouldn't want to stand in a toilet, it's most —'

'YOU DON'T HAVE TO STAND IN THE TOILET!' Dad suddenly yelled, tearing at his hair. 'YOU SIT ON THE TOILET! THEN YOU TAKE A SHOWER.'

Granny looked at Dad steadily. 'You always were a noisy child,' she told him. 'And I still don't see why I should have to sit on the toilet if I want a shower. When I want a shower at home I don't –'

'YOU'RE NOT AT HOME. THIS IS A CAMPER VAN!' Dad howled.

'Just look at him,' said Granny, shaking her head. 'You'd think he was three, wouldn't you?' She glanced at the beds, counting them. 'There's only room for five to sleep. Where do Lancelot and I go?'

Dad turned red. 'You're not coming,' he said tetchily. 'I mean, I was just thinking of the family.'

'But we *are* family. I'm your mother,' Granny pointed out. She caught my eye and winked at me. She was winding Dad up.

'I know,' Dad grumbled. 'I mean *family* family – Brenda and Nicholas and me and the twins.'

'And Poop!' added Cheese.

'Oh yes, you must take Poop,' said Granny, quickly.

'How many more times? We are not taking Poop!' Dad couldn't take much more.

Cheese began punching the air with one hand, then the other and he marched round, shouting, 'Pooper-dooper, sooper-pooper!'

Then Lancelot joined in, tucking his hands under his armpits and flapping his elbows and strutting round the van like a chicken. 'Prrrarkk! Prrrarrrkk! We're going camping!'

'Right, that's it,' grumbled Dad.

'I've had enough. I'm taking the camper van back and we're going to stay at home and twiddle our thumbs and not go anywhere at all.'

Mum slipped an arm round Dad's waist. 'Oh, stop being such a misery-guts. Don't you know when you're being teased? Your mother's pulling your leg. Of course she and Lancelot aren't coming camping with us. They'll be here, looking after Rubbish.'

Dad's frown vanished. 'Oh, right. I'd forgotten about that.'

So there we are, we're going on a camping holiday and I can't wait!

5 Who's Taking What?

We packed most of the van yesterday. It's got
loads of cupboards and places to put things. It's
really clever. The cupboard doors and drawers
have special locks on them to stop them opening
when we're driving along. The beds pack down
and turn into proper seats. The fridge even has
an ice-maker.

We're going away for a week and I had to
choose all the clothes and things I wanted to
take. Mum helped Cheese and Tomato. Tomato
wanted to take the wheelbarrow for Cecily
Sprout but Mum told her it was too big. Then
Cheese carried Poop upstairs, put the hen in his
bag and did up the zip so that just Poop's head
was sticking out.

'No,' said Mum, in her stern voice. Cheese scowled, stuck his hands on his hips and looked defiant for several seconds while he and Mum had a silent staring match. Finally, he unzipped the bag, lifted Poop out and went stamping back downstairs. There was something about the look on his face that made me think we hadn't seen the last of Poop.

Meanwhile, Tomato was carefully packing her carrot. Cecily was wearing Barbie pyjamas for the journey.

'I'm sure Cecily is going to love camping,' smiled Mum.

'She says she won't like it if it rains,' Tomato warned.

'It won't rain. It's going to be lovely and hot. Has Cecily got a swimming costume?'

'Yes,' nodded Tomato. 'She's got a blue bikini and sunglasses but she mustn't go in the sun too much in case she burns.'

Mum glanced at me and bit her bottom lip very hard to stop herself from laughing out loud. I guess we were both imagining a carrot with sunglasses, not to mention the bikini.

Dad had packed three suitcases, and that was just for him.

'What have you put in there?!' quizzed Mum.

'Scuba-diving kit, inflatable dinghy, five pairs of trousers, sixteen shirts, eight jumpers, three jackets, ten pairs of shoes, socks, underpants, pyjamas, slippers, toothbrush, books to read and the goat.' Dad saw the look on Mum's face. 'Just joking about the goat,' he added quickly.

'Well, I hope you're joking about the scuba-diving kit and the dinghy and all those clothes too. We're only going away for a week. We're not moving house!'

Dad scratched his head. 'Do you think it's too much?'

'Of course it's too much. If we put all that in the van there won't be any room left for people. You are allowed one case only, one small case.'

'What about the –' began Dad.

'Leave it,' Mum interrupted. 'If you have to ask you obviously don't need it. I suggest you take two of everything.'

'Does that mean two shoes, or two pairs of shoes?'

'Of course I mean two pairs. Why would you only take one shoe? What's the point?'

Dad shrugged. 'I was just asking. Sometimes women say strange things.'

'That's probably because sometimes men *do*

strange things,' Mum shot back. 'Especially in this house. Nicholas, how is your packing going?' Mum checked through my bag and nodded approvingly. 'You'd better go and help your father,' she suggested. 'Thank heavens you're sensible.'

I grinned and went to help Dad. What this actually meant was that I stood on the bed and gave him orders while Dad held things up for my inspection. 'Yes. No. No. No. That's my old teddy. Why have you got my old teddy?'

Dad turned a deep red. 'I like it,' he muttered.

'You'll have to leave it behind. No. Yes. No. No. Dad, you've shown me your scuba-diving kit three times now and I've said "no" each time.'

'I was hoping you might forget you'd already said "no" and say "yes" instead.'

'The answer is still "no",' I ordered.

'Spoilsport,' Dad complained, and so we went on.

Mrs Tugg has agreed to look after the chickens. She said that she's not going to tell her husband until we've actually gone, because otherwise he'll make a fuss.

'He's never been fond of animals since he was a child,' she confided to Mum. 'His dad took him to the zoo. He was standing next to the monkey cage while his dad took a photo and a monkey came up and pulled on his trousers and they fell down round his ankles.'

'Oh dear!' laughed Mum.

Mrs Tugg was chuckling too. 'I know! It was

rather embarrassing, of course, but things like
that seem to happen to him.'

I didn't get to bed until late and even then I
couldn't sleep. I was too excited. I have no idea
what time it was when I eventually dropped off,
but Cheese woke me up in the morning. Or to
put it another way, Poop woke me up. She was

squawking loudly because Cheese was trying to stuff her into my bag. He was determined that the hen was going to go camping.

'You can't put Poop in there,' I said. 'Mum will find out and she'll be cross. Poop can't come with us.'

Cheese stood there with Poop tucked under his arm and they both stared at me in silence. Even the hen seemed to be looking daggers at me. Cheese stuck his thumb into his mouth and walked off without a word.

We had a quick breakfast, then loaded a few last things into the camper van. Mum gave the vehicle a final search.

'What are you looking for?' asked Dad.

'A certain small, brown, fluffy creature,' hinted Mum. 'You know how stubborn Cheese gets sometimes. OK, we appear to be without Poop. We can go.'

Brilliant! We were on the road at last and our first camping holiday had begun. The van decided to celebrate by letting off an enormous, farty BANG, jumping in the air and dying on the spot.

'Dad?' I panicked.

'It's all right, Nick, nothing serious. It's probably the carbo-petrolio-plugga-doo-bit.'

Mum fixed him with a steely glare. 'You don't know what it is, do you?'

'Yes, I do. It's – the van.'

'Which bit of the van?' Mum demanded.

'Er, a big bit,' Dad ventured. He turned

the key in the ignition once more. There was
another huge BANG! The entire van leaped
in the air as if it had just been stung by a
helicopter-sized wasp. The engine burst into
life. We were off – again! I can't wait to see the
campsite.

6 Bitten by a Duck

We're on the campsite and Poop is here too!
Guess where Mum found her? Cheese had
smuggled her into the camper van and hidden
her inside the little oven! It was the one place
Mum never thought to
look. She was quite cross at
first but there was nothing
she could do about it. I
think that secretly she
thought Cheese had been
pretty clever, and he had
too. He was beaming all
over his face.

Dad said it was lucky the
oven hadn't been turned

on. 'Otherwise poor Poop really would be a chicken nugget by now.'

'You have a sick sense of humour,' grunted Mum.

'I didn't put the hen in the oven,' protested Dad. 'I was only saying.'

I have never seen so many tents and caravans. There are titchy, tiny tents and there are tents the size of a castle. Some of them even have an upstairs bit. No, just kidding! But they are definitely enormous, and all colours – red, green, brown ones and blue ones. Some people even have stripy tents and one tent has a skull and crossbones flag flying outside. They must be pirates on holiday.

Some of the caravans are so big they've got six wheels. They have TV and aerials and everything. One of them even has a jacuzzi. That's what Dad said, and I saw a woman WASHING HER TENT this morning. She was, really. I mean – washing a *tent*? That is weird!

Cheese has made a friend here, a boy called Lewis. I think he's four or five. He's a bit on the tubby side and he's got a dull face that looks like wet pastry. His parents are in one of the posh caravans. Cheese showed his new friend our camper van.

'It's very small,' said Lewis, so my little brother showed him the toilet. He even showed him how to lift up the seat.

'It's very small,' sniffed Lewis.

'And it's a shower,' Cheese added.

'Our shower doesn't have a toilet in it,' Lewis boasted. 'It's a proper shower and you can stand up.'

Cheese pressed on gamely and showed Lewis the beds. 'That's where I sleep and my sister, and Nicholas sleeps here and Mum and Dad sleep there.'

'I've got my own room,' Lewis said airily. 'And so have my mum and dad.' He gazed round the van. 'It's very small,' he said for the third time.

I was fed up with this. 'I know it's small,' I said. 'But we're small people.'

'No, you're not. You're bigger than me,' Lewis said flatly.

'We shrink at night,' I told him. Lewis looked at me carefully. I could tell he was trying to imagine me shrinking.

'How small do you get?' he asked at last, and I smiled.

'About the size of a cat.'

Lewis was silent. Hooray. That had shut
him up for the time being. Then he saw Poop
sitting on top of the fridge unit. Lewis eyed her
suspiciously.

'Is that your duck?' he asked.

'She's a hen, not a duck. She's called Poop.'

But Lewis had lost interest. He'd just spotted
something even more unusual. 'That carrot is
wearing sunglasses and a bikini.'

'Yes,' I said.

'Why?'

'Because the sun's shining and it's hot,' I answered.

'She's called Cecily,' Cheese announced. 'Cecily Sprout.'

'That's a stupid name for a carrot,' said Lewis, and I thought that actually it's a stupid name for *anything*, let alone a carrot. Besides, what's a *sensible* name for a carrot, apart from *carrot*?

'It's Tomato's doll,' I told him.

'Who?'

'Tomato,' I repeated.

'My sister,' said Cheese.

'They're twins,' I added.

Lewis looked deeply puzzled, as well he might. I knew this was a struggle for him. Poor kid – I was overloading him with odd information. First the hen, then the carrot, and now the Pizza Twins.

'Cheese and Tomato?' Lewis repeated hoarsely.

I nodded and eventually Lewis gave up thinking about it and moved on to safer material. 'We've got a dog,' he boasted. 'He's called Henry. It's a proper name. Henry is a big dog.'

'Oh. So let's see, you've got a big caravan and a big shower and a big bedroom and a big dog?'

'And a big television and a big car and a big daddy,' Lewis put in for good measure.

'My dad's big,' Cheese remarked.

'Not as big as my dad,' Lewis shot back. 'His tummy hangs right over his trousers. My mum calls him Mr Hippo.'

'Lovely,' I murmured, glad that my dad wasn't a hippo. He's more like a chimpanzee really.

'We're going to the safari park this afternoon. They've got lions and tigers and elephants and seals and zebras and monkeys and ice creams and Dad said I can have five scoops on mine and it will be the biggest ice cream in the world.'

'What a surprise,' I muttered.

'We're going too,' announced Cheese, even

though we weren't. His eyes were popping. I knew he'd love to go. I'm going to talk to Mum and Dad about it later and maybe they'll take us.

Cheese lifted up Poop and held her out to Lewis. 'You can hold her,' he said. Lewis took the hen but she began to squawk and flap and finally she flew up into his face, knocking him over.

'Your duck bit me!' Lewis squawked, picking himself up.

'Hen,' I corrected. 'They don't bite. You held her too tightly. She doesn't like being squeezed.'

'I'm going to tell my mum,' said Lewis.

'OK,' I smiled. 'Tell your mum a duck bit you and see what she says. Bye.'

Lewis ran off towards his caravan.

'Lewis is a big boy,' Cheese declared proudly. It reminded me of when I was four or five and I wanted to be friends with the big boys. I'm not like that now, of course, but I knew how Cheese felt. It was just a shame that my little brother had picked the awful Lewis.

7 Ice Screams

Mum thinks that going to the safari park is a brilliant idea.

'Cheese thought of it,' I said, and Mum ruffled my brother's hair. Dad said that Granny had taken him to a safari park when he was a child.

'I remember we went on a boat on a lake to watch the seals. I leaned over the side to see them better and I dropped my ice cream. It landed slop-plop on a seal's head.'

'Dad! What did the seal do?'

'Nothing. Another seal ate it.'

'Bad seal,' said Cheese.

'You haven't changed much, have you?' said Mum.

'What do you mean?' asked Dad.

'You were having daft accidents then and you still have daft accidents now,' she pointed out.

'No, I don't!'

'Ron, just a few nights ago you were running round the hen house in the middle of the night with a child's tent stuck round your waist.'

Dad reddened. 'Yes, but that was a special occasion.'

'I should hope so too! And last week you were nailing down that bit of carpet in our bedroom and you put a nail through a central heating pipe and caused a flood. And when you cooked supper the other night you left the chocolate puds in the oven and they bubbled up and spilled all over the bottom. It took me two hours to clean it and the puds had to be thrown out. And last month you –'

'La-la-la-la-la-la, can't hear you!' sang Dad, holding up his hands. 'I think we should all go to the safari park right now this minute.'

'Are you trying to change the subject?' Mum asked with a smile.

'Of course I am,' grinned Dad. 'Come on, everyone in the van and, no, Cheese, Poop is not going to sit with us. She might start flapping about and get in the way. She'll have to go back in the oven. Come on, hop in and let's go. And

I forbid anyone to mention any more accidents that I've had.'

Mum turned and smiled at us.

The safari park isn't far from the campsite and we soon joined a queue of cars as they slowly entered the park. We kept passing signs that said things like:

DO NOT FEED THE ANIMALS.

DO NOT OPEN YOUR CAR WINDOWS.

DO NOT GET OUT OF YOUR CAR.

IF YOUR CAR BREAKS DOWN,

WAIT FOR ASSISTANCE.

IF A TIGER OPENS ITS MOUTH

DO NOT CLIMB INSIDE.

No! I made that last one up!

It was pretty good and Cheese and Tomato thought it was amazing. Tomato held Cecily Sprout up to the window and shouted out the names of the animals she saw. 'Look, Cecily! There's a pig!'

'It's a rhinoceros, darling,' Mum said.

'A crockerator! You can see all its teeth!'

'Crocodile,' said Mum. 'Or maybe an alligator. They look much the same and I can't read the sign from here.'

'I think crockerator is a rather good name,' chuckled Dad. 'It reminds me of Crunchbag. Do you remember?'

'How could we forget?' laughed Mum. 'That alligator you brought home almost destroyed the house, not to mention Mr Tugg's car.'

Cheese joined in with the animal spotting, shouting right in my ear and almost deafening me. 'There's a pencil! And another one – lots of pencils!'

'Penguins,' I snorted. 'Not pencils.'

'I wonder if they have a lake here,' Dad mused. 'The leaflet says they've got seals.'

'Yes, they do,' said Mum. 'There's the sign for it pointing down that track. They have boat rides too. Does this mean you want to feed the seals with your ice cream again?'

'Ice cream!' yelled Cheese, deafening me again. 'Five scoops!'

'Five?' repeated Mum. 'Your eyes are bigger than your stomach, young man.'

I told her what Lewis had said and Mum's eyes widened. 'Yes, well obviously some parents are a bit silly.'

I kept quiet. I'd been

planning to ask for five scoops myself. We got
to the lake and, sure enough, there was an ice-
cream stall next to the ticket office for the boat.
We all got an ice cream because Dad insisted.

'Don't you dare drop it again,' said Mum.

'I won't. I'm going to tape the scoops on to the
cone to make sure they don't fall off.'

'Dad! You can't tape ice cream!' I laughed.

'Really? Oh, all right, I'll nail them on then. Now, where's the nearest seal?'

He was joking of course and we climbed on to the little boat and had a fun ride round the lake. The seals swam up to the boat and honked and splashed Tomato, which made her laugh but then her ice cream fell into the water. A seal ate it and Cheese thought it was so funny he threw his ice cream into the water on purpose and a seal ate that too. The twins screamed with delight.

Mum and Dad were not impressed. 'We didn't buy ice creams so that you two could feed the seals,' complained Mum. 'It's your fault, Ron, telling them silly stories about when you were a child.'

Dad began to protest and splutter but he couldn't think of where to start. Eventually he turned to me and raised his arms in disbelief. 'All my fault again,' he murmured, 'and I haven't even done anything!'

After that it was decided that we ought to head home. Cheese fell asleep in the van and Tomato played hide and seek with her carrot, which meant she hid the carrot and then found her . . . umpteen times.

And guess what was waiting for us when we got back to the

campsite? Granny and Lancelot! And guess who they had with them? Rubbish, our goat!

8 A Volcanic Eruption

'They didn't want to let us in,' Granny explained. 'They said "You can't bring a goat in here!" And Lancelot said oh yes we could because they have a sign that says PETS WELCOME.' Granny looked at her husband and her eyes twinkled. She slipped an arm through his. 'He's my hero!'

'Mother, please!' Dad winced. 'Not in front of the children.'

'And this babe's my princess!' declared Lancelot, planting a kiss on Granny's cheek. It was a bit

embarrassing, and I don't mean the kissing, I mean calling my gran 'babe'. She's sixty-seven!

'Anyway,' Granny went on, 'the man at the gate said goats didn't count as pets and weren't allowed. So Lancelot said that he had a friend who had a pet camel, and some people kept poisonous snakes as pets, and goats weren't as big as camels or as dangerous as poisonous snakes and Rubbish was a pet. Then he gave the man a ten-pound note and he let us in.'

'Has your friend really got a pet camel?' I asked Lancelot. He grinned back at me.

'Yes, he has. Mind you, the camel is made of wood and it's only fifteen centimetres tall, but I didn't tell the man on the gate that!' Lancelot burst out laughing.

'But why did you decide to come camping all of a sudden?' Mum asked Granny.

'I guess we just got a bit bored, dear, sitting at home. The sun was shining and we thought of you all enjoying yourselves and suddenly realized that we could come too. Now then, Nicholas, you must come and see our tent.'

'Is it special?' I asked and she shook her head.

'Speckled? No, I don't think so.'

'I said "special", Granny, not "speckled".'

'Oh, well, yes, it is rather special. Come on.'

We followed Granny and Lancelot to the other side of the campsite and there we found an extraordinary tent, with Lancelot's big three-

wheeler chopper motorbike parked next to it.
Several people had gathered round and were
staring, goggle-eyed, at both the tent and the
bike.

The tent was circular, with a round, pointed
roof made from proper wooden rafters, and it was
pretty big. The most amazing bit was when you
went inside. It had four different areas marked
out, like little rooms. One was for cooking,
one was for living in and the other two were
bedrooms. The canvas walls were decorated with

strange pictures and designs. The main room didn't have any chairs, but just a low platform covered with rugs and cushions. The whole tent looked like some magical place straight out of an Arabian fairy tale like *Sinbad* or *Aladdin*.

'It's a yurt,' Lancelot announced proudly. 'And it's the only one on the campsite. In fact it's probably the only yurt for miles around. Pretty big too – we had to bring it on the three-wheeler.'

'It's fabulous!' I breathed, while Cheese and Tomato happily threw themselves at the cushions and bounced off.

'It is rather romantic,' sighed Mum.

'Give me a proper tent any day,' grunted Dad.

'Yes,' laughed Mum. 'You go back to your little play-tent, Ron. You'll be safe there. I don't know about anyone else, but I could do with a cup of tea.'

'Oh dear,' muttered Gran. 'I haven't had a chance to go and get any milk yet.'

'Squeeze the goat,' suggested Dad.

'I can't take you anywhere,' Mum murmured. 'We've got plenty of milk at our van. Let's head back there.'

No sooner had we returned than Tomato burst into tears. 'Can't find Cecily!' she wailed. 'Cecily Sprout has gone.'

'Oh, darling, that's so sad,' said Mum. 'Where did you lose her?'

'I don't know.'

'Were you playing hide and seek with her again?'

Tomato shook her curls. 'No. I wasn't playing anything.'

'Let's check the van. I hope you didn't leave her at the safari park?'

'She couldn't have,' I pointed out. 'She was playing with the doll on her way back this afternoon.'

We turned the van inside out but all we found was a tomato that reminded me of Mr Tugg – red and bald. There was no carrot in a bikini.

'We shall have to scour the campsite,' sighed
Mum, taking Tomato's hand. Tomato frowned
fiercely at the rest of us.

'We ALL have to look,' she ordered, so the
whole family set off on a Cecily hunt, with
Tomato calling out the carrot's name at regular
intervals as we searched the campsite. 'Cecily?
Cecily Sprout!'

Other campers heard us and wanted to know

what was going on. Soon Tomato had half the
campsite wandering about shouting out 'Cecily
Sprout!' at the tops of their voices. I guess they
thought it was a real person that had gone
missing – not just a carrot with green stalks for
hair and wearing a blue bikini.

In the middle of all this a small car drove
furiously up to our tent. The door was flung
open and out stepped Mr Tugg, our next-door

neighbour, the human volcano, and he was already in full eruption.

'There you are!' he roared at Dad. 'I've got something for you!' He reached into the back of the car and pulled out two wire cages. Inside I could see Captain Birdseye, Mavis Moppet, Beaky and Leaky. They looked mildly surprised, as if they'd just been caught spraying graffiti on Mr Tugg's shed. Schumacher the tortoise was in

there too, fast asleep.

'What's the matter, Mr Tugg?' asked Mum. 'You seem upset.'

'Upset? Of course I'm upset. Do you know what your wretched chickens did yesterday evening? They invaded our house. That's right – invaded it.'

'But how? I mean, why?' Dad asked, puzzled.

'That fox of yours came back!' bellowed Mr Tugg.

'It's not *my* fox,' Dad put in swiftly. 'Foxes don't belong, they're just, well, foxes.'

Mr Tugg was too worked up to pay any attention to Dad. 'That fox of yours scared the hens so much they all ran into my house. Your cock-a-doodle-dumbo there knocked over my wife's aromatherapy cabinet and then walked up and down Mrs Crossbottom's back just when she was having a quiet massage session with my wife. It was the shock of her life! She jumped up and ran into the garden.'

'A lucky escape,' Dad ventured.

'Not lucky at all!' roared Mr Tugg. 'She had nothing on! And I was out there gardening! I didn't know where to look!'

'Oh dear, I should think her bottom *was* very cross after that,' said Dad, who was beginning to enjoy this. He always seemed to find it funny when Mr Tugg got angry.

'And then the fox came *inside* the house and chased the hens upstairs. They've left feathers all over the place, not to mention the unmentionable. One of them jumped out of the window and landed on Mrs Crossbottom's head and that set her off again. She'll never come back and the house is wrecked. Wrecked! So here are your wretched beasts and you'd better not bring them back, ever. You can pay for all the damage. I'm writing to the council about this, and your pesky goat and pesky tortoise.'

Dad reddened. 'What on earth has the tortoise done? Eaten your house?'

'NO! MY BEST PRIZE-WINNING BEGONIAS, YOU IDIOT! I hope they arrest you and put you in prison – and your hens too. Good afternoon!' Mr Tugg leaped back into his car, gunned the engine and roared off across the grass.

Dad looked at Mum. Mum looked at Dad.
Granny looked at Lancelot and Lancelot looked
at me.

'Oh dear,' we chorused.

9 And Here's Henry . . .

Gloom, gloom, gloom. For several minutes we stood there, hardly exchanging a word, while the hens quietly clucked and glanced at us from time to time, like naughty children. The small crowd of campers that had gathered to watch Mr Tugg's performance drifted away. It was Mum who spoke first.

'I thought we came on holiday to escape the farm but somehow they all seem to have ended up here too – Rubbish, the hens, the tortoise. I'm surprised Mr Tugg didn't bring all our lettuces and carrots too.'

'That man's a fool to himself,' growled Dad. 'All he had to do was keep his doors and windows shut.'

Cheese and Tomato arrived back from the hunt for Cecily Sprout. They had Lewis in tow. Tomato had been crying and was still sniffing a bit.

'You didn't find her?' asked Mum. Tomato shook her head.

'It's a stupid doll,' Lewis stated. 'It's a carrot.'

'A parrot?' asked Granny. 'No, dear, these are hens. Parrots are quite different. They have bigger beaks and longer tails and they can talk, some of them. When I was a little girl my uncle had a parrot that used to say "Doughnuts made of dynamite are a deadly danger to Dodos".'

Lewis looked around for help. He obviously thought Granny must come from outer space.

I took Tomato's hand. 'Let's go and play a game,' I suggested.

'What – *sniff* – game?' she asked.

'We can play Catch the Duck!' shouted Lewis, diving towards the hens. Lancelot just managed to grab Lewis before he could open a cage.

'No you don't, laddie,' said Lancelot firmly. 'Those animals are hens and they're pets.'

'Put me down or I'll tell my mum!' shouted Lewis, waggling his legs and trying to wriggle free. Lancelot put him back on the ground and scratched his head.

'I used to be a Hell's Angel,' he murmured, giving me a pathetic look. 'I'm supposed to be scary.'

I laughed. Lancelot is about as scary as a teddy bear.

'I'm sure someone can think of a good game to keep you all busy,' he suggested hopefully.

'You could play safari park,' I said, and Cheese and Tomato and even Lewis began to shout like crazy.

'Yeah! Safari park! We can play safari park! Hooray!' They began jumping about and laughing until they suddenly stopped and Tomato looked at me solemnly.

'How do we play safari park?' she wanted to know.

Lancelot and Granny looked at me too. 'Yes, Nicholas. Do tell us. How do you play safari park?'

I shrugged. I didn't know. It was just a kind of idea that popped into my head when I saw the hens and Schumacher. Then I had a thought – maybe that was it! 'We've got a goat and a tortoise and some chickens. You can pretend they're animals in your safari park and you have to look after them. You must make sure they have enough to eat and they don't run away.'

'Yes!' shouted Lewis. 'And we all have to wear caps!'

'Caps?' repeated Mum in bewilderment.

'I think he means like a zookeeper or something,' I suggested.

'I'm in charge of the goat,' Lewis declared. He seemed to think that because he was the biggest child he should have the biggest animal. I thought that was unfair, but Dad smiled broadly and said that of course Lewis could look

after the goat. Dad winked at me. He knew
perfectly well that Rubbish wouldn't let *anyone*
look after her. She had a mind of her own and
did what she wanted.

Granny said that the three safari park officers
could have their safari park outside their yurt.
'There's more room over there,' she pointed out.
'Come on. You come too, Nicholas. You can
help keep an eye on things and then your mum
and dad can have a bit of peace and quiet for a
change.'

I love Granny and Lancelot's yurt. It's amazing. It's SO different from the other tents and caravans. Loads of people stop to stare at it. Some of them even ask if they can have a tour inside.

We carried all the animals across to the yurt. We didn't carry Rubbish, of course; she trotted after me. She often follows me around because I'm the one that usually milks her. Lancelot let the chickens out so they could peck over the ground and showed Lewis how to hold Mavis Moppet without squeezing her like bagpipes.

'This is a good safari park,' said Tomato, who seemed to have forgotten all about the disappearance of Cecily Sprout.

'We should have lions and tigers and a big snake,' complained Lewis.

'What would you put in the lake, dear?' asked Granny.

'What lake?' Lewis gazed around.

'The lake you just mentioned,' Granny smiled.

Lewis's mouth dropped open but he couldn't think what to say.

'He said *snake*, babe, not lake,' laughed Lancelot, shaking his head.

'Oh! I do beg your pardon!'

Lewis looked at her blankly. It was impossible to tell what he was thinking, or even if he was thinking at all. He was, because he suddenly announced that there should be some proper big animals in the safari park.

'You've got a goat,' Lancelot pointed out.

'We can have my dog, Henry,' Lewis said. 'He's big.' Before we could say anything Lewis had dumped Mavis Moppet and run off to his parents' caravan. Cheese watched him go.

'Lewis has got a big dog,' he told us proudly. 'It's this big!' Cheese stretched as high as he could, exaggerating as usual.

'That's huge!' I laughed. 'That would be a giant dog.'

Cheese nodded. 'Yes. Henry's a giant, giant, GIANT dog.'

At that moment I spotted Lewis walking slowly back towards us. He had his father with him,

and Henry. My eyes almost fell out of my head.
Henry really was a big dog, and I mean he was
BIG, the most gigantic dog I have ever seen,
practically as tall as ME!

10 A Small Victory

'Henry is an Irish Wolfhound,' Lewis's father smirked. 'Wolfhounds are the tallest dogs in the world. There's no need to be scared. Henry is as gentle as a lamb and very well behaved.'

Henry spotted the hens and decided he wanted to sniff them. However, Captain Birdseye didn't want to be sniffed by a dog the size of a lorry, and I can't say I blamed him. The cockerel uttered a shrill squawk and flapped in Henry's face. Henry barked a lot and Rubbish looked at the dog angrily and decided it was time to act.

The goat lowered her head and charged. The hens scattered in fear, flying and flapping in all directions. Henry leaped out of the goat's path, whirled round and galloped after her. Rubbish

skidded to a halt and charged back at him.
Meanwhile the rest of us were trying to gather
up the chickens and the air was filled with a
rising chorus of squeaks, squawks, grunts, growls,
barks, bleats and, quite suddenly, the awful sound
of tearing canvas. Henry and Rubbish had just
ploughed straight through someone's tent.

97

'Get out!' screamed a bearded man, whirling his arms in the air so hard I thought he might take off. The dog and the goat went careering off and soon they were carving their way through one tent after another, leaving a trail of destruction. It wasn't long before the entire campsite was up in arms, yelling and screaming and hurtling after the two beasts, both of whom now had bits of tent flapping about them like strange flags.

'Stop them!'

Lancelot and Granny leaped on to their motorbike and went roaring off after the two maddened animals. Granny was driving and Lancelot was standing – yes, standing! – on the seat, giving directions. As they caught up with the

thundering pair Lancelot leaped from the bike
and hurled himself on to the wolfhound. They
crashed to the ground, rolling over and over.
Henry had been captured.

Rubbish skidded to a halt and turned to see
what had happened. A crowd gathered round
and began to press in. She looked at them
nervously and kept lowering her head as if she
was going to charge. I seized the moment and

grabbed someone's washing-up bowl. I crawled between everyone's legs until I came out into the little circle where the goat was now standing. Rubbish had managed to spear a large section of tent with one of her horns and she had someone's shopping bag draped over the other.

'It's OK, Rubbish,' I said quietly.

'You watch out, sonny,' growled Lewis's father. 'That goat's a killer.' Someone in the crowd suggested she should be shot.

'Don't listen to them, Rubbish. Everything's all right.' By this time I was right next to her. I scratched her between the ears. She likes that. She closed her eyes several times. She has such amazing, long eyelashes – you should see them! I patted her back gently, slipped the basin between her legs, squatted down and began milking her.

'Heavens above!' cried somebody. 'Take a look at that. The boy's milking her!'

'Don't be daft,' snapped Lewis's dad. 'Milk comes from cows.'

'And goats,' the woman next to him said. 'My father has a farm. He keeps goats for milk.'

'That's disgusting,' muttered Lewis's dad.

'All mammals make milk,' a child's voice said. 'We learnt about that at school.'

'All mammals?' queried Lewis's father, who was having great difficulty accepting the revolutionary idea that it wasn't just cows that produced milk. 'Even mice?'

'Yep,' said the boy.

'Elephants! Ha! I bet elephants don't make milk.'

'Of course they do,' said the boy.

'OK then, how about squirrels?'

'Yep.'

Lewis's dad's shoulders slumped and he shook his head in disbelief. Gradually the crowd moved away, all except for the people whose tents had been ripped apart. They wanted to know what the campsite owner was going to do about all the damage. We soon discovered the answer to that, because he threw all of us off the site! He told Lewis's family to leave as well. They were furious and said it was all our fault.

'But your dog chased our goat and hens!' said Dad.

'You shouldn't have a goat!' growled Lewis's father. 'Whoever heard of anyone taking a goat camping? A milk-squirting goat? It's revolting, and you can take your horrible carrot as well. I found my son playing with it. Your family's weird – fancy putting a carrot in a bikini.'

Lewis's father practically threw Cecily Sprout at Mum. So that was what had happened to Cecily. Lewis had kidnapped her! Tomato was over the moon. 'Mummy, mummy! Cecily Sprout has come back! She went to play with that big boy!'

'I wasn't playing with her,' snapped Lewis, turning bright red.

'Your dad said you were,' nodded Cheese.

Lewis huffed and puffed, not sure what to do or say. At last his eyes settled on Rubbish, and a smug smile crept on to his pudgy face. 'Anyway,' he said, 'your goat is stupid.' And he marched off with a toss of his head.

For a moment Cheese watched him go. Then he ran after Lewis, stopped him, looked straight at the older boy and folded his arms across his little chest.

'I think,' my brother said firmly, 'I think your dog is very, VERY BIG!'

'Huh. Of course he is, stupid. He's the biggest dog in the world,' Lewis sneered.

'Yes,' agreed Cheese. 'He is very, VERY BIG, but he is VERY STUPID!'

Lewis's eyes bulged. Cheese sensed that he'd gained an advantage and pressed on with his withering attack. 'And so are YOU!' he finished off.

I hurried over and took Cheese by the hand before Lewis decided to launch an attack of his own. A five-year-old battling with a three-year-old would not be much of a contest at all.

'Come on, Cheese,' I said. 'You need to pack your toys before we go.'

Lewis gazed after us, clenching and unclenching his fists. It was only a small victory, but Cheese and I enjoyed it an awful lot. Not only that, but Tomato had been reunited with Cecily Sprout. However, it didn't change the fact that we had to leave. We'd only been camping for three days.

We're back home now and I don't think it's the end of our problems. There was a letter from the council waiting for Dad. They'd received

Mr Tugg's complaint and they're coming to investigate. If they don't like what they find they can tell us to get rid of all our animals. It's not fair.

11 Startling Events

It was such a muddled afternoon yesterday that
we forgot to have any supper. We didn't get home
from the campsite until the evening and then we
had to unload the car, settle the hens back in the
coop, milk Rubbish AND water the vegetable
patch. I don't think I'll be a farmer when I grow
up. There's too much looking after to do. I mean,
you even have to look after cabbages and lettuces
and stuff!

I was so tired by the time all that had been
done I went straight to bed. It was only when I
woke in the middle of the night that I realized
how hungry I was. I tried to get back to sleep but
my tummy felt as if several mice were nibbling
away inside it. My bedside clock said quarter

past two. It was hours before breakfast. I'd die of starvation before then! The only thing to do was to get up and creep downstairs, trying not to wake anyone, and find something to eat.

If you've ever gone on a food hunt in the middle of the night you'll know what it's like. There are all those floorboards and stairs that squeak and creak. The noise sounded like thunder to me, but everyone slept on. Dad was snoring quietly. At least, I think it was Dad. I suppose it might just as easily have been Mum.

I got to the kitchen safely and hunted around for some food. I decided to have a whopping bowl of cereal because it was easy to sort out. I fetched a bowl, filled it up and got some milk from the fridge. Then I sat down at the kitchen table and began to chomp my way through it all. Wow! There's nothing like a midnight feast – magic!

Outside, the hens started clucking, which was odd because it was still dark. I know Captain

Birdseye likes to crow early in the morning, but half past two is way too soon for him. I was sort of eating and looking out of the kitchen window at the same time and that was when I saw the figure in our garden, down near the hen house.

Whoah! I was so shocked I dropped my spoon. It fell into my bowl making the biggest splosh ever. My hands automatically shot out to try and catch it and I managed to catapult it right out of the bowl instead, flicking milk in my face and all down my pyjamas. Nice one, Nicholas. Why don't you drown yourself in milk!

The spoon fell to the floor and clattered on to the tiles. Whoever it was in the garden turned and looked towards the house as if they'd heard something. I ducked down and stayed there a few seconds. Then I crept closer to the window to get a better look. I was beginning to wonder if it was Mr Tugg out there, creeping about, but if it was, what was he up to?

When I saw the figure climb over our fence

and into next-door's garden I was sure it was Mr
Tugg. He was obviously heading home. Mind
you, he seemed to be having a lot of difficulty
getting into his house and was struggling with the
back door. Eventually he gave up and decided to
try a window instead.

A WINDOW?!

IT WASN'T MR TUGG AT ALL!

IT WAS A THIEF!

I was about to rush upstairs to wake Dad when the burglar alarm went off. At least what actually happened was that the chickens went off. They were the alarm! They suddenly went berserk, led by their choirmaster, Captain Birdseye. You should have heard the shrieks!

A moment later Mr Tugg's searchlights fizzed on and the gardens were flooded with light. The burglar froze in panic, staring all around and then decided to make a run for it in our direction. With one bound he cleared the fence and began to sprint across our vegetable patch before he skidded to a halt and stared in horror at the creature in front of him.

It was the fox! The fox had returned for the hens and now the burglar had caught the fox red-handed and the fox had caught the burglar red-handed and the pair of them stood and stared at each other, with the fox snarling and spitting furiously, showing all his very sharp teeth.

The burglar decided to beat a hasty retreat.

He charged back towards Mr Tugg's garden,
leaping our fence for the third time, and landed
– SPLASH – in the middle of the Tuggs' pond.
He crawled out only to find Mr
Tugg standing over him, blowing
his whistle and waving his
Neighbourhood Watch
badge at him.

Seconds later my mum and dad appeared in the garden, wondering what was going on, and then Mrs Tugg came hurrying out from next door. She threw her arms round her husband and said that she had never seen such bravery. Mr Tugg went red with embarrassment.

'What happened?' asked my dad, still half asleep.

Mr Tugg smiled. Whoopee! It felt like Christmas! Mr Tugg actually looks quite cuddly when he smiles. 'Just for once you haven't been the cause of all this mayhem,' he said with some satisfaction. 'I have just caught a burglar. The police are already on their way. It's quite safe now,' he went on airily. 'You can go back to your beds and sleep soundly. Everything's under control.' Mr Tugg drew himself up to his full height and gave a self-satisfied nod. 'All under control.'

Dad shook his head and turned to go back indoors. 'That's fine then. Goodnight, officer.'

'Goodnight,' nodded Mr Tugg.

We got back inside and I had to tell Mum and Dad every detail of what had happened. My parents had big bowls of cereal while I told them because by this time they were hungry too. (And I had another bowl because, if you remember, most of my first bowl was sprinkled across the kitchen floor.) We went back to bed and I slept in until ten o'clock in the morning. Brilliant!

We had to get Granny and Lancelot round so we could tell them in the morning. We were halfway through all that when the doorbell rang. It was the inspector from the council. She'd come to inspect our garden – and we'd clean forgotten all about it because of last night.

'There have been several complaints from your neighbour Mr Tugg,' said Miss Rice, with a sniff.

'What a surprise,' muttered Dad.

'I understand you keep hens here, and a goat and a tortoise?'

'That's right.'

'I'd like to see them, please.'

Tomato suddenly burst into the room, waving a rather mangled carrot. 'Cecily Sprout fell down the stairs and she's brokened her leg!' she cried.

'Oh dear, that is sad,' murmured Mum soothingly.

'Look!' said my sister, holding up her doll. One of the carrot's two pointy legs had snapped right off. Her green hair had gone rather limp and brown too.

'A carrot has a broken leg?' Miss Rice gave my father such a look of alarm that he quickly steered her outside and showed her the garden.

'It's quite a little farm you have here,' Miss Rice said with surprise. 'Now tell me, how loud are your animals?'

Dad shrugged. 'The hens cluck, Captain Birdseye crows, Rubbish bleats and the tortoise keeps himself to himself.'

'Yes, but how loud are they? Can you make them squeak for me?'

'Not really, no,' answered Dad. 'It's not the sort of thing you do with farm animals – make them squeak. Normally you just feed them, milk them or collect eggs.'

Miss Rice shook her head. 'That's not good enough. I need to hear how loudly they squeak. Can't you poke them?'

'Poke them?' echoed Dad. 'Are you mad?'

Oh dear. I could see which way things were going and I desperately hoped Dad would keep his cool. It wasn't going to happen, of course.

'No, I am not mad at all. I need to hear your

animals being noisy. That's my job. If you won't poke them, I will. Give me that stick.'

'No, I shan't,' said Dad. 'Nobody is allowed to poke my animals, not even me. How would you like it if I poked you?' Dad grabbed the stick. Oh no! I shut my eyes. I knew what was going to happen next.

'Just a moment!' a voice bellowed. I opened my eyes again. It was Mr Tugg. He called over the fence. 'Miss Rice! How lovely to see you. Before you go any further I wonder if I might have a word? I'm the one who has complained

about these animals. Now, as captain of the local Neighbourhood Watch, some recent developments have come to my attention.'

'Oh, you'd like to add to your complaints, would you?' asked Miss Rice, getting out a notebook.

'No, not exactly.' Mr Tugg began to scratch his head as if he had taken himself by surprise. 'In fact I would like to withdraw all my complaints.'

'All of them?' chorused Miss Rice and Dad, for quite different reasons.

'Yes. Last night I caught a burglar, and it was entirely because of these hens. If they hadn't made such a fuss I wouldn't have woken up. You see, the hens acted as a burglar alarm. Without them, the thief would have broken into our homes. I'm very grateful to them.'

'Really?' chorused Dad and Miss Rice, for quite different reasons again.

'Oh yes. So please drop the matter,' smiled Mr

Tugg. 'In fact I'd like to make the hens my official nightwatchmen, or rather nightwatch-hens.'

And that was that! Miss Rice has gone and we can keep Rubbish and Schumacher and, of course, Captain Birdseye, Mavis Moppet, Beaky, Leaky and Poop. It's brilliant! And the biggest surprise of all came when Mum went to the hen house a bit later.

'The hens have laid!' she yelled back to the house. 'They've all laid eggs, every one of them!'

So that made it double brilliant. And guess what? We're going camping again in a couple of weeks. Dad says we'll go to a different campsite, and we're not going to take any animals. Tomato seems to have forgotten all about Cecily Sprout. She's now waiting excitedly for the eggs to hatch. She seems to think that they are going to produce kittens.

'Because that's what I want,' she told me. 'Four kittens – a tabby, a ginger one, a white one and a

pink one.'

'Pink?' I repeated.

'Yes. And I'm going to call it Pink-Poop, because I like pink and I like Poop.'

I guess that once you've lived with a carrot called Cecily Sprout, Pink-Poop seems like a pretty good name.

14½ Things You Didn't Know About

Jeremy Strong

★ ★ ★ ★ ★ ★ ★ ★ ★ ★ ★ ★ ★ ★ ★ ★ ★

1. He loves eating liquorice.

2. He used to like diving. He once dived from the high board and his trunks came off!

3. He used to play electric violin in a rock band called **THE INEDIBLE CHEESE SANDWICH**.

4. He got a 100-metre swimming certificate when he couldn't even swim.

5. When he was five, he sat on a heater and burnt his bottom.

6. Jeremy used to look after a dog that kept eating his underpants. (No – NOT while he was wearing them!)

7. When he was five, he left a basin tap running with the plug in and flooded the bathroom.

8. He can make his ears waggle.

9. He has visited over a thousand schools.

10. He once scored minus ten in an exam! That's ten less than nothing!

11. His hair has gone grey, but his mind hasn't.

12. He'd like to have a pet tiger.

13. He'd like to learn the piano.

14. He has dreadful handwriting.

And a half . . . His favourite hobby is sleeping. He's very good at it.

Ask Jeremy

Of all the books you have written, which one is your favourite?

I loved writing both **KRAZY KOW SAVES THE WORLD – WELL, ALMOST** and **STUFF**, my first book for teenagers. Both these made me laugh out loud while I was writing and I was pleased with the overall result in each case. I also love writing the stories about Nicholas and his daft family – **MY DAD**, **MY MUM**, **MY BROTHER** and so on.

If you couldn't be a writer what would you be?

Well, I'd be pretty fed up for a start, because writing was the one thing I knew I wanted to do from the age of nine onward. But if I DID have to do something else, I would love to be either an accomplished pianist or an artist of some sort. Music and art have played a big part in my whole life and I would love to be involved in them in some way.

What's the best thing about writing stories?

Oh dear – so many things to say here! Getting paid for making things up is pretty high on the list! It's also something you do on your own, inside your own head – nobody can interfere with that. The only boss you have is yourself. And you are creating something that nobody else has made before you. I also love making my readers laugh and want to read more and more.

Did you ever have a nightmare teacher?
(And who was your best ever?)

My nightmare at primary school was Mrs Chappell, long since dead. I knew her secret – she was not actually human. She was a Tyrannosaurus rex in disguise. She taught me for two years when I was in Y5 and Y6, and we didn't like each other at all. My best ever was when I was in Y3 and Y4. Her name was Miss Cox, and she was the one who first encouraged me to write stories. She was brilliant. Sadly, she is long dead too.

When you were a kid you used to play kiss-chase. Did you always do the chasing or did anyone ever chase you?!

I usually did the chasing, but when I got chased, I didn't bother to run very fast! Maybe I shouldn't admit to that! We didn't play kiss-chase at school – it was usually played during holidays. If we had tried playing it at school we would have been in serious trouble. Mind you, I seemed to spend most of my time in trouble of one sort or another, so maybe it wouldn't have mattered that much.